Bei
First Day
of First Grade

BE BIG!

written by Katie Kizer

Book
Design by
yipjar.com

*To my nieces, Ava and Lyla, and to all the women
in my life who have shown me how to be big.*

K.K.

STORYBOOK
GENIUS PUBLISHING
sbgpublishing.com

yipjar Book
Design by
yipjar.com

The day had finally arrived. Beatrice had waited, and wanted, and dreamed all summer long for this.

It was the first day of first grade!

In honor of first grade,
she put on her favorite **BLUE** tutu!

Beatrice sat down
for breakfast in the little kitchen,
in the tiny apartment, in the gigantic city where she lived.
With each spoonful, Beatrice thought more...and more...
...about what first grade would be like.

What if my teacher isn't nice!

What if I get lost?

What if something goes wrong?

"You can't wear your tutu to school, Beatrice.
You're not a kindergartener anymore,"
said Beatrice's brother.

Beatrice had worn her BLUE tutu every day that summer.
It was her favorite thing in the whole world.
But she didn't want to stick out, either.

Beatrice took off her tutu
and threw it in the toy bin.

Just then, out of the corner of her eye, Beatrice saw something move.
She looked up to find a tiny butterfly flying right through her window!

"Hi!" said the butterfly.
"I'm Benjamin. I got lost in your garden and I can't find my friends. May I stay with you until I find them?"

Beatrice couldn't bear the thought of the tiny butterfly all alone. And first grade wouldn't be so scary with a secret friend by her side.

"Of course! You can come with me to first grade!" she said.

Off Beatrice went
to first grade...

...with Benjamin following close behind.

The first day of first grade was going pretty well for Beatrice until it was time for read-aloud circle.

Beatrice was confused about something the teacher had read, so she wanted to ask a question.

"But I'm afraid to sound silly," she whispered to Benjamin. "What if one of your classmates has the same question? **BE BIG!** Raise your hand high!" said Benjamin.

So Beatrice raised her hand.

When it was time for arts and crafts,
all of the other children were busy working...

...all but Beatrice.

"I have an idea for a drawing, but I'm afraid it won't look right," she whispered to Benjamin.

"What if your drawing inspires others? **BE BIG!** Draw something you love!" said Benjamin.

So Beatrice drew her **BLUE** tutu.

On the playground,
a few children were starting
a game of leapfrog, and Beatrice
wanted to play, too.

"But I'm afraid they won't want to play with me,"
she whispered to Benjamin.

"What if you're the person who would make the game complete?
BE BIG! Jump into the leapfrog fun!" said Benjamin.

So Beatrice jumped in!

The first day of first grade was over!
It turned out to be a very good day for Beatrice!

"Let's go home, Benjamin," Beatrice said.

On their walk home, Beatrice noticed that Benjamin looked sad.

"What is wrong, Benjamin?" Beatrice asked.

"I had a wonderful first day of first grade with you... but I miss my friends," Benjamin said just as he was interrupted by voices coming from the garden!

"Beatrice! Look! You helped me find my friends!" said Benjamin.

"I am happy you found your friends!" Beatrice said. "Thank you for going to the first day of first grade with me, Benjamin."

"You are very welcome, Beatrice. I am glad you decided to **BE BIG**, today!"

"Remember, it's okay to be afraid and be yourself anyway. Chances are, you're not alone," Benjamin said as he gave Beatrice a kiss goodbye.

The next morning, Beatrice went to her second day of first grade wearing her BLUE tutu!

How have you been **BIG**?

What can you do to feel big?

BeBIG!

Come explore more at TheBeBigBook.com

CPSIA information can be obtained
at www.ICGtesting.com
Printed in the USA
BVHW091409120819
555678BV00013BA/86/P